Hello Kitty

Happy Birthday!

© 1976, 2014 SANRIO CO., LTD
First published in the UK by HarperCollins *Children's Books* in 2014
1 3 5 7 9 10 8 6 4 2
ISBN: 978-0-00-754560-5

Written by Neil Dunnicliffe
Designed by Anna Lubecka

www.harpercollins.co.uk

Printed and bound in China

Hello Kitty

Happy Birthday!

HarperCollins *Children's Books*

Hello Kitty loves birthdays.
Today is extra-special -
it's Hello Kitty's own birthday!

She can't wait to have
lots and lots of fun!

The postman arrives with a
bumper postbag. There are lots
of lovely cards for Hello Kitty.

Dear Daniel has sent an extra-large card!
It's almost as big as Hello Kitty!

Mummy has planned a special party
to celebrate Hello Kitty's birthday.

There will be lots of scrummy food, party games, decorations, music and more!

Daddy is wrapping
Hello Kitty's present.

There seems to be more glitter on Daddy than there is on the present!

The house has been decorated with balloons, bunting, streamers and posters.

Careful you don't sit
on that balloon, Hello Kitty!

Hello Kitty's friends have all received invitations to the party. They're so excited!

Dear **Fifi** ....

You are invited to
Hello Kitty's
Birthday Party

This Saturday
at 3pm

Dress code:
Party time!

Hello Kitty is planning what to wear. So many options!

What should she choose?

Ding Dong!

Ding dong goes the doorbell.
The guests arrive, looking very happy.

They all shout "Happy Birthday!"

Everyone is wearing
a colourful party hat.

Who do you think
looks the silliest?

There are lots of party games, including musical statues.

Who do you think will move first?

It's time for the birthday cake!
It looks delicious.

Don't forget to make a secret wish
when you blow out the candles, Hello Kitty!

All the friends
sing to Hello Kitty.

They make
a very loud noise!

It's present time! Hello Kitty has
received lots of lovely things.

which do you think is her favourite?

Hello Kitty thinks that
the best present of all...

is spending the day
with her friends and family.

HAPPY BIRTHDAY
HELLO KITTY!

The world of

Hello Kitty

Enjoy all of these wonderful Hello Kitty books.

Picture books

Occasion books

Where's Hello Kitty?

Activity books

...and more!

Hello Kitty and friends story book series

KINGFISHER

First published 2018 by Kingfisher
an imprint of Macmillan Children's Books
20 New Wharf Road, London N1 9RR
Associated companies throughout the world
www.panmacmillan.com

Authors: Jacqueline McCann and Emma Dods
Design and styling: Liz Adcock
Cover design: Liz Adcock
Illustrations: Marc Aspinall

ISBN 978-0-7534-4335-4

9 8 7 6 5 4 3 2 1

1TR/0418/WKT/UG/140WFO

A CIP catalogue record for this book is available from the British Library.

Printed in China

Wow!
Animals

A Book of Extraordinary Facts